Summerbath

Winterbath

Written by
Eileen Spinelli

Illustrated by
Elsa Warnick

EERDMANS BOOKS FOR YOUNG READERS

GRAND RAPIDS, MICHIGAN   CAMBRIDGE, U. K.

Text copyright ©2001 Eileen Spinelli
Illustrations copyright ©2001 Elsa Warnick
Published 2001 by Eerdmans Books for Young Readers
An imprint of Wm. B. Eerdmans Publishing Company
255 Jefferson Ave. S.E., Grand Rapids, Michigan 49503
P.O. Box 163, Cambridge CB3 9PU U.K.

www.eerdmans.com/youngreaders

Library of Congress Cataloging-in-Publication Data
Spinelli, Eileen
Summerbath, winterbath / written by Eileen Spinelli;
illustrated by Elsa Warnick
p.cm.
Summary: In summer and in winter,
Althea enjoys the ritual of taking her bath.
ISBN 0-8028-5179-7 (cloth : alk. paper)
[1. Baths — Fiction.] I. Warnick, Elsa, ill. II. Title
PZ7.S7566 St 2001
[E] — dc21
00-055095

The illustrations were done in watercolor.
The text was set in Venetian.

To my happy-splashing nieces and nephews
— *E. S.*

To my sons Matt and Milan Erceg,
whose spirits inspired these images.
— *E. W.*

Long ago,
    when garden spiders were fat
    and summers strawberry scented,
       Althea was a child.

On Saturday mornings

    Althea's father would carry a metal washtub to the backyard.

    He filled the tub with water from the pump.

    The water was cold.

    All day the tub of water sat in the warm sun . . .

all day, while Althea ran barefoot with her cousins . . .

stopping at noon to pick peppers and beans for her mother . . .

then chasing after the iceman's wagon,
tiny winter on wheels,
begging for chips of shaved ice.

Before supper

    Althea rocked her baby brother on the porch swing

        so her mother could roast the chicken in peace.

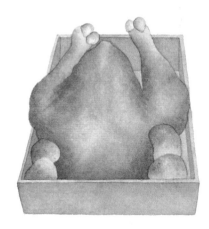

After supper,

when stars and fireflies spilled into the night

and the backyard was a puddle of moonlight,

Althea pulled on her black woolen bathing suit.

Her mother handed her a chunk of brown soap,
and Althea scrubbed and splashed in the backyard tub,
in the daylong, sunwarmed water,
singing with tree frogs and crickets,
singing a summerbath song.

When winter came,

    mice skittered from backyard to kitchen.

        Snow sifted like flour through the window cracks.

Althea and her cousins played marbles and jacks on the floor . . .

stopping at noon for bowlfuls of lentil soup,
steaming and thick.

They scoured the pot with ashes
till they could see their faces in it.

Before supper
　　Althea pulled her baby brother
　　　　around the bedroom in a dishpan

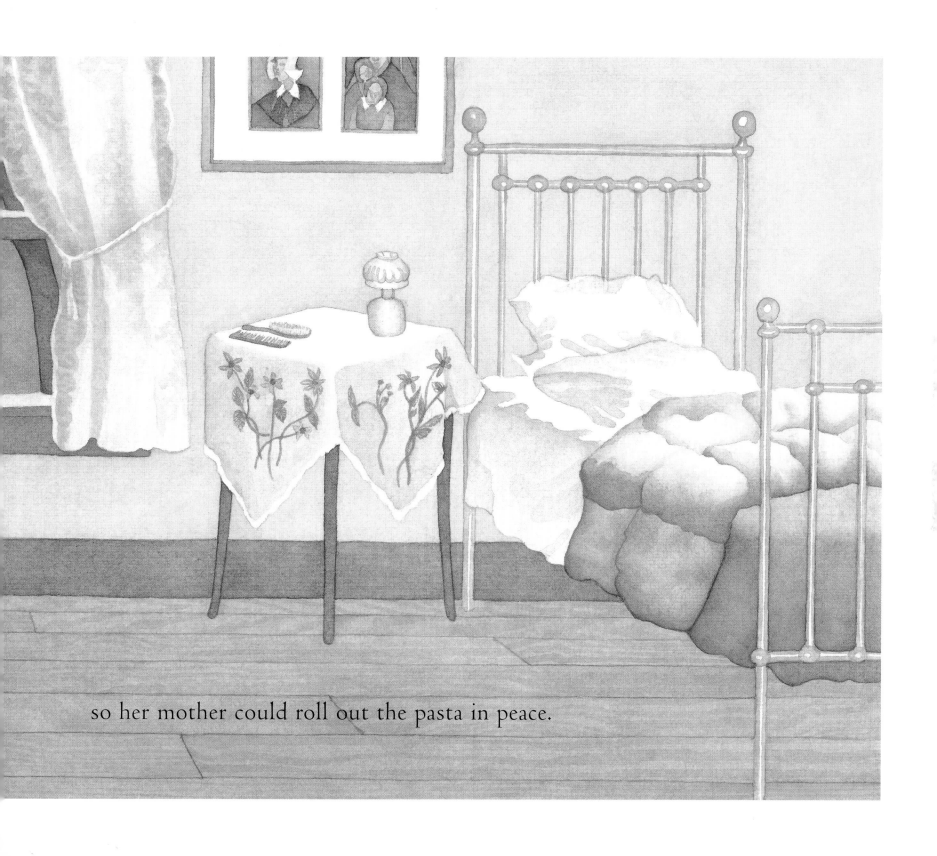

so her mother could roll out the pasta in peace.

After supper

    Althea's father added wood to the fire in the stove.

    Althea's mother heated water in kettles,

        filled the metal washtub,

            and tested the water with her elbow.

She hung sheets across the kitchen.

Behind the sheets
   Althea splashed in the summerwarm water,
      hummed with the whispering wind,
      whistled with the distant train
         her winterbath song.

Long ago,
    when streets were cobblestone
    and gas lamps winked
    at the winter moon

    and Althea was a child.